This book belongs to

_____

D0503164

© 2006 Big Idea, Inc.

VEGGIETALES®, character names, likenesses, and other indicia
are trademarks of Big Idea, Inc. All rights reserved.

All scripture quotations, unless otherwise indicated, are taken from the
HOLY BIBLE, NEW INTERNATIONAL READER'S VERSION®.
Copyright © 1995, 1996, 1998 by International Bible Society.
All rights reserved.

Published by Scholastic Inc., 90 Old Sherman Turnpike, Danbury, Connecticut 06816.

No part of this work may be reproduced in whole or in part, or stored in a retrieval system,
or transmitted in any form or by any means, electronic, mechanical, photocopying, recording,
or otherwise, without written permission of the publisher.

SCHOLASTIC and associated logos are trademarks and/or
registered trademarks of Scholastic Inc.

This product is available for distribution only through the direct-to-home market.

ISBN: 0-7172-9926-0

Printed in the U.S.A.

First Scholastic printing, April 2006

THE GOOD, THE BAD, AND THE SILLY

A Lesson in *Making Good Choices*

by
Doug Peterson

Illustrated by
Tom Bancroft
and Rob Corley
Colored by Jon Conkling

SCHOLASTIC INC.

New York Toronto London Auckland Sydney
Mexico City New Delhi Hong Kong Buenos Aires

Bong! The clock struck high noon.

Cowboy Larry was shakin' in his boots—it was the day of his big cattle-drive test at Cowboy School.

Sheriff Bob, the cattle-drive teacher, glanced at the names on his clipboard.

"Next up: Cowboy Larry, Botch Scallion, and the Sunburn Kid," he said.

Cowboy Larry's heart pounded like a hammer. It was his turn!

In this test, Cowboy Larry would have to move 40 cows from one ranch to another. If he could do it fast enough, he would pass with flying colors. But he would have to work as part of a team. And his partners would be none other than those rascals Botch Scallion and the Sunburn Kid.

"Howdy, partners," Cowboy Larry said to Botch and Sunburn.

Botch snarled, as crabby as a cowpoke with a cactus in his pants. But the Sunburn Kid didn't answer at all. He was too busy trying to cover his belly with sunscreen.

Splurt! The sunscreen splattered Cowboy Larry in the nose instead. "Oops—sorry!" said the Sunburn Kid.

Cowboy Larry **really** wanted to pass the cattle-drive test. After all, he didn't do very well on his advanced-moseying test the week before.

"You know how it works, boys," said Bob. "You've got to move those cows from the Okie-Dokie Corral and around Dodge Ball Canyon. Get the cows to the Ranch Dressing Ranch before sundown and you pass."

"Sounds good. Let's round 'em up!" shouted Cowboy Larry, but Botch just growled. The Sunburn Kid didn't say a word, because he was too busy putting T-shirts on the cows—to keep the sun off their backs.

The cattle-drive test started out wonderfully. Cowboy Larry rode alongside the cows, shouting cowboy things like "Rollin', rollin', rollin', keep them doggies moving!"—even though they were cows and not dogs.

But as they neared Dodge Ball Canyon, Botch led the cattle off the trail. He took the cows down into the canyon.

"Uh . . . Mr. Botch, aren't we supposed to take the cows *around* Dodge Ball Canyon?" asked Cowboy Larry.

"This is the shortcut," muttered Botch.

"But cutting through Dodge Ball Canyon would be cheating," said Cowboy Larry.

"So what? You got a problem, boy?"

"Well . . . yeah," Cowboy Larry said. "God has a problem with it, too."

"But cheating gets good grades," said Botch. "Isn't that true, Sunburn?"

The Sunburn Kid didn't answer.

Cowboy Larry knew that taking a shortcut through Dodge Ball Canyon wouldn't just be cheating—it would be dangerous. Mountain lions prowled the canyon. And if they made too much noise, they could trigger a deadly avalanche of dodge balls.

"Are you coming or not?" asked Botch.

DODGE BALL CANYON! BEWARE! DANGER! DO YOU HAVE MOUNTAIN LION INSURANCE?

Cowboy Larry wasn't sure what to do. Should he do the **good** thing and say he won't go along with the others? Should he do the **bad** thing and follow Botch and the Sunburn Kid? Or should he do the **silly** thing and help Sunburn put hats and sunglasses on all the cows to protect their eyes from dangerous ultraviolet rays?

"C'mon," snarled Botch. "Who's even gonna know we cheated?"

"Well . . . okay," said Cowboy Larry. He decided to follow Botch and the Sunburn Kid, but Cowboy Larry felt rotten about it.

So they led the cows into the deadly Dodge Ball Canyon. Buzzards circled overhead. Lizards lay out in the sun. Tumbleweeds blew by. And the Sunburn Kid nearly got bit trying to put sunscreen on rattlesnakes.

SUN SCREEN

Grrowwl!

"What was that?" asked the Sunburn Kid, gulping and glancing around.

"Don't worry," snarled Botch, even though he knew it might be a growling mountain lion.

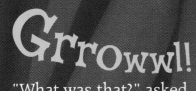

Grrrowwl!

"There it is again," gasped Sunburn. "I don't like this, Botch!"

By this time, Cowboy Larry knew he had made the wrong choice. He shouldn't have decided to cheat. But he also realized that it wasn't too late to change his mind. It's never too late to do the **good** thing.

"You asked who's going to know if we cheat," Cowboy Larry said to Botch. "Well . . . *I'll* know. And so will God. So I'm turning around. Are you coming or not?"

"Good riddance," grumbled Botch. *"Adiós, amigo."*
But as Cowboy Larry rode out of Dodge Ball Canyon,
Botch and the Sunburn Kid suddenly heard it again.

Grrrrrowwwwwl!

Botch rolled his eyes. "That isn't a mountain lion growling," he said to Sunburn. "That's your *stomach* growling."

"Gee, I think you're right," said Sunburn. "I knew I should've ordered *three* flapjack breakfasts this morning at Clint's Covered Wagon Café."

Grrrrrrowwwwwwwll!

Cows are not especially smart. The more they heard Sunburn's stomach growling, the more afraid they became. They were sure it was the sound of growling mountain lions.

Finally, one of the cows couldn't take it any longer. Terrified, she ran! And when one cow bolted, all of them did.

"*Stampede!*" shouted Botch.

Wildly out of control, the cattle thundered across the land, kicking up dust. They shook the ground like an earthquake. The result?

"Avalanche!" exclaimed the Sunburn Kid.

Thousands of dodge balls came crashing down from the hills, burying the cowboys in bouncy rubber balls.

Cowboy Larry got out of the canyon just before the avalanche happened. When the dust settled, he was able to gallop back and throw a rope to Botch and Sunburn. He pulled them and the cows out from under the dodge balls.

Yippie Ki Yea, Ki Yea! Cowboy Larry had saved the day!

"Good thing I didn't stay with you guys," he told Botch and Sunburn. Cowboy Larry had learned to follow God, rather than follow the crowd—or the herd.

It was dark by the time they returned to the Okie-Dokie Corral. Miss Kitty,
the Cowboy School owner, handed root beers to the tired cowboys.

"I'm sorry," said Sheriff Bob. "I can't give you your Cattle-Drive License today."

Cowboy Larry was as happy as could be. Although he didn't pass the cattle-drive
test, he had passed a more important test. He didn't cheat.

Cowboy Larry had made the **good** choice after all.

The Sunburn Kid, meanwhile, didn't mind that they had failed. Night had fallen in the Wild, Wild West, and he was too busy smearing "moonscreen" on his face.

Splurt!

"Oops—sorry!" he said to Cowboy Larry.

Do not follow the crowd when they do what is wrong.
Exodus 23:2